This edition published by Parragon Books Ltd in 2016

Parragon Books Ltd
Chartist House
15–17 Trim Street
Bath BA1 1HA, UK
www.parragon.com

ISBN 978-1-4748-5064-3

Printed in China

BEDTIME TALES

Bath • New York • Cologne • Melbourne • Delhi
Hong Kong • Shenzhen • Singapore

Contents

The Magic Sky

One icy Arctic night, Lila and Poko the polar bear cubs were getting ready for bed. It was freezing outside, but it was cosy and warm inside their den. The two cubs snuggled down beside their mother and closed their eyes. They were almost asleep, when they heard a noise outside.

"Psst! Lila! Poko!" said a voice. It was their friend Tiki the Arctic hare.

"Come outside! Quickly!" whispered Tiki. "There is something I want to show you. Something very peculiar is happening. I think there must be magic in the air."

"What's going on?" yawned Mother Bear sleepily.

"Something magical is happening," replied Tiki. "I can't describe it. You must come and see for yourself."

"Ah," smiled Mother Bear. "I think I know what it is. Let's all go and take a look together."

The three sleepy polar bears crawled out of their den and padded across the icy snow. Lila and Poko looked around in surprise. Everything looked so different.

The icy landscape was bathed in a strange glow.

"Look up," whispered Tiki.

The polar bear cubs looked up and gasped in amazement.
Something very strange was happening in the sky above.
It was full of dancing lights, swirling and twirling around
above their heads. They all stared in wonder, unable to speak
at first.

"It's beautiful!" gasped Poko eventually.

"What's happening?" asked Lila.

"It's the Northern Lights!" said Mother Bear.

"Is it magic?" asked Poko excitedly. "We love magic."

Mother Bear thought for a while and then smiled.

"Yes," she agreed. "It's the magic of nature!"

The Three Billy Goats Gruff

Once upon a time, there lived three billy goat brothers. There was a big billy goat, with a great big belly and great big horns. There was a middle-size billy goat, with a middle-size belly and middle-size horns. And there was a little billy goat, with a teeny little belly and teeny little horns.

All three were brave and all had deep, gruff voices, so they called themselves the Billy Goats Gruff.

The three Billy Goats Gruff lived on a hill beside a bubbling river. Across the river was a meadow full of sweet, juicy clover – the goats' favourite food. The goats longed to visit the meadow, but to get there they had to cross a small, rickety wooden bridge.

The Billy Goats Gruff would have happily crossed the small, rickety bridge if it hadn't been for one thing – the meanest, fiercest troll you could possibly imagine lived beneath it. His eyes burned like fire and his warts bristled with thick, dark hairs. He had slimy fangs for teeth and claws as sharp as razor blades. He was always, always hungry and his favourite food was . . . GOAT!

Few dared cross that bridge, and those that did were never heard of ever again. The Billy Goats Gruff were brave goats, but not stupid, so they stayed away from the bridge and ate the grass in their field. They ate and ate and ate, until one day there was nothing left but dirt.

As the goats looked across the river to the sweet, juicy clover on the other side, their bellies rumbled. Eventually, when they could bear it no more, they decided that they had no other choice but to cross the bridge.

"I'm not scared of that ugly troll," said the little Billy Goat Gruff. So he decided to go first.

The little Billy Goat Gruff's hooves clip-clopped over the bridge. He hadn't gone far when there was a terrifying ROOOAR and the ugly troll leaped out.

"Who's that clip-clopping over my bridge?" roared the troll.

"Only me, the teeny little Billy Goat Gruff," replied the smallest billy goat bravely. "I'm on my way to the meadow to eat some sweet, juicy clover."

"Oh, no, you're not," bellowed the troll. "I'm hungry, and I'm going to gobble you up."

"Please don't do that," replied the brave little Billy Goat Gruff.

"I'm just small and bony. My brother will be coming this way soon. He is far bigger and juicier than me. And he'll make a much better meal."

The troll licked his lips hungrily. He hadn't eaten in a few days but decided he could wait just a little longer if it meant his next meal was even bigger.

"You do look kind of scrawny," he said slowly. "Perhaps I could wait just a little longer for a bigger meal. Now shoo, before I change my mind."

So the little Billy Goat Gruff skipped across the bridge and was soon munching on the sweet, juicy clover on the other side.

Not long afterwards, the middle-size Billy Goat Gruff began clip-clopping his way across the bridge.

"Who's that clip-clopping over my bridge?" snarled the troll.

"Only me, the middle-size Billy Goat Gruff," replied the next billy goat. "I'm on my way to the meadow to eat clover."

"Oh, no you're not," snarled the troll. "I'm going to gobble you up!" And the troll opened his mouth wide, ready.

"Please don't do that," replied the middle-size Billy Goat.

"If you wait a little longer, my big brother will be crossing your bridge. He's got a great big belly and will fill you up in no time at all."

The troll rubbed his huge, round belly greedily. Maybe it wasn't so bad to wait just a bit longer for an even bigger meal.

"Okay," he said finally, "I'll wait for the big billy goat." And he let the middle-size billy goat go.

It wasn't long before he heard a loud clip-clopping sound. The big Billy Goat Gruff was on his way.

"Who's that clip-clopping across my bridge?" roared the troll.

"Just me, the biggest Billy Goat Gruff of all," cried the last billy goat. And before the troll could say a word, he lowered his horns and charged at the troll.

SMACK – the big Billy Goat butted into him and tossed him high into the air. SPLASH! He landed in the water and disappeared.

Then the big Billy Goat Gruff clip-clopped across the bridge to join his brothers in the meadow full of sweet, juicy clover.

And as for the silly old troll? Well, he was never seen ever again!

The Fox and the Crow

One day, a crow was flying past an open window when she spotted a tasty piece of cheese on the table. There was no one in the room, so she fluttered in and stole the morsel. Then she flew up into the branches of a nearby tree, and was just about to eat it when a fox appeared.

The fox was particularly fond of cheese and he was determined to steal the crow's prize.

"Good morning, Mistress Crow," he greeted her. "May I say that you are looking especially beautiful today? Your feathers are so glossy, and your eyes are as bright as sparkling jewels!"

The fox hoped that the crow would reply and drop the cheese, but she didn't even thank him for his compliments. So he tried again: "You have such a graceful neck, and your claws are really magnificent. They look like the claws of an eagle."

Still the crow ignored him.

The fox could smell the delicious cheese, and it was making his mouth water. He had to find a way to make the crow drop it. At last he came up with a plan.

"All in all, you are a most beautiful bird," he said. "In fact, if your voice matched your beauty, I would call you the Queen of Birds. Why don't you sing a song for me?"

Now, the crow liked the idea of being addressed as the Queen of Birds by all the other creatures in the woods. She thought that the fox would be very impressed by her loud voice, so she lifted her head and started to caw.

Of course, as soon as she opened her beak the piece of cheese fell down, down, down to the ground.

The fox grabbed it in an instant and gobbled it up.

"Thank you," he said. "That was all I wanted. I have to say that you may have a loud voice, but you don't have a very good brain!"

Aesop's moral: Never trust a flatterer.

Why Owls Stare

Once upon a time there lived an owl and a pigeon.
They were friends, but they were great rivals too,
and they were always boasting to one another.

"Owls have much better eyesight than pigeons," the
owl would claim.

"Pigeons are much better at flying," the pigeon would reply.

"Owls have better hearing," the owl would brag.

"Pigeons have prettier feathers," the pigeon would argue.

One morning they were sitting side by side on a branch when
the owl said, "I think there are many more owls than pigeons."

"That can't be right," replied the pigeon. "There are
definitely far more pigeons than owls. There's only one way to
find out. I challenge you to count them!"

"All right," the owl agreed. "We will need a place with plenty
of trees. Let's do it in the Big Wood a week from today. That
will give us time to let everyone know."

During that week the owl and the pigeon flew in
every direction to tell their fellow birds to come to the
Big Wood to be counted.

The day of the count came, and the owls were the first to
arrive. It seemed as if every tree was full of owls
hooting at each other.

There were so many, the owls were sure they would outnumber the pigeons.

Suddenly the sky went dark. Clouds of pigeons were flying towards the Big Wood. They came from the north, the south, the east and the west. Soon there was no space left in the trees, and branches were starting to break under the weight of all the pigeons.

More and more pigeons came, circling above the wood, looking for a place to land. By now, the ground was completely covered with pigeons, too. The owls were wide-eyed with amazement as they stared at all the pigeons, who were still arriving by their thousands. The noise of their wings was deafening, and the owls were getting squashed and trampled by the ones who had managed to find a perch in the trees.

"Let's get out of here," the owls hooted to one another, flying away. But the poor creatures had stared so long and hard at the pigeons that their eyes stayed stuck wide open – and from that day on owls always stared, and hid during the day when the pigeons were nearby, flying only at night.

Goldilocks and the Three Bears

Once there was a beautiful little girl called Goldilocks, with gleaming golden hair. But although she looked like an angel, Goldilocks didn't behave like one. She was often naughty, and didn't do as she was told.

One day, Goldilocks went out to play.

"Stay close to home," her mother reminded her. "Don't go into the forest, or you will get lost."

At first, Goldilocks did as she was told. But then she started to get bored. "Why shouldn't I go into the forest if I want to?" she muttered to herself. "I won't get lost if I stay on the path."

When her mother wasn't looking, Goldilocks skipped across the meadow and into the forest. She had so much fun, she forgot about staying on the path. It wasn't until her tummy began to rumble that she realised she was lost.

"Drat!" she said. "I'm hungry!"

Suddenly, Goldilocks caught a whiff of something yummy.

"Hhhmmm!" she sniffed. "That smells delicious."

The smell led Goldilocks to the door of a small house.

She knocked loudly.
RAT-A-TAT-TAT!
"I don't see anyone," said
Goldilocks, peeking in through the
window. "They must be out."
So she opened the door and
marched right in.

On the kitchen table were three
bowls of sticky, syrupy porridge:
a great big one, a middle-size one
and a teeny-weeny one.

In an instant, Goldilocks dipped a
spoon into the biggest bowl and slurped the porridge hungrily.
"Ouch!" she spluttered. "That's too hot!"

Next she tried the middle-size bowl of porridge. YUCK!
It was much too cold. So Goldilocks dipped her spoon into the
teeny-weeny bowl and tasted it. YUM! It was just right.
She gobbled it all up quickly!

When she had finished licking the syrupy spoon, Goldilocks
looked around the room. There were three comfy chairs by the
fire: a great big one, a middle-size one and a tiny one.

"Just the place for a nap," yawned Goldilocks sleepily.
She flopped down onto the biggest chair.

"Ouch!" she yelled, jumping up. "That's too hard!"

The middle-size chair was even worse. It was much too soft.

So Goldilocks tried the tiny chair. It was very small, but finally she managed to squeeze herself onto the seat. Suddenly, there was a loud SNAP! then CRASH! Goldilocks fell to the floor in a heap of broken chair legs.

Then Goldilocks saw a staircase in the corner of the room. At the top, she found a room with three beds in it: a great big one, a middle-size one and a tiny one.

"I'll just lie down for a little while," Goldilocks decided. So she bounced onto the biggest bed. OOF! It was much too lumpy. Then she bounced onto the middle-size bed. FLUMP! "Too squashy!" she giggled, rolling off.

Goldilocks sat on the tiny bed and tried a little bounce. It was just right, so she lay down. Soon she was fast asleep. She didn't know the owners of the house were coming home.

The owners of the house were a family of bears: a big daddy bear, a middle-size mummy bear and a tiny baby bear! As soon as they got home, the bear family went straight to the table to eat their breakfast ...

"Who's been eating my porridge?" growled Daddy Bear.

"And who's been eating my porridge?" growled Mummy Bear.

"At least you've got some left!" cried Baby Bear. "Look! Mine's all gone. Even the spoon is licked clean!"

Daddy Bear looked around the room. "Who's been sitting in my chair?" he growled.

"Who's been sitting in my chair?" growled Mummy Bear.

"At least you've still got a chair!" cried Baby Bear. "Look! Mine's all broken!"

The three bears went upstairs.

"Who's been lying on my bed?" growled Daddy Bear.

"And who's been lying on my bed?" growled Mummy Bear.

"At least there's no one in your bed!" cried Baby Bear.

At that very moment, Goldilocks woke up and saw the three bears. At first she thought she was dreaming. But when the biggest bear growled,

"WHO ARE YOU?"

she knew it wasn't a dream. She leaped up, ran down the stairs, and did not stop until she reached home.

And from that day on, Goldilocks changed her ways. Not only did she look like an angel, but she tried to behave like one, too. Well... most of the time!

The Lion and the Mouse

One day, a lion was fast asleep in his den when he was woken by something running across his face. The lion lazily opened one eye and was surprised to see a little mouse right in front of his nose. As fast as lightning, the lion's paw shot out and caught the mouse.

"How dare you run across the face of the king of beasts!" the lion roared. "You will pay for that with your life!"

The lion opened his enormous mouth and was just about to swallow the mouse, when he heard the creature squeaking.

"Please don't eat me, sir," the mouse pleaded. "If you forgive me and let me go, I will do something for you one day, to repay your kindness."

The lion laughed and laughed at the thought that a creature as small and unimportant as a mouse could ever do anything to help the king of beasts.

"You repay me?" the lion spluttered. "I can't imagine that."

But, because the lion had just eaten a big meal and he found the mouse's plea so funny, he let the little creature go.

Some time later, the lion was stalking a zebra when he became caught in a net that had been laid on the ground by hunters. The lion tried to free himself, but the more he struggled, the more he got tangled in the ropes. Soon, he was too exhausted to struggle anymore, or even roar for help.

The lion had almost given up hope of ever escaping, when who should come by but the little mouse he had let go earlier.

"Let me help you," squeaked the little mouse, climbing onto the lion's shoulder. And he began to nibble through the ropes with his sharp teeth. Soon he had bitten through most of the knots, and the lion wriggled free.

Before running off, the lion thanked the little mouse.

"I am very grateful to you, my friend," he said. "You have taught me an important lesson: no act of kindness is wasted, however small it may be."

Aesop's moral: Little friends can turn out to be great friends.

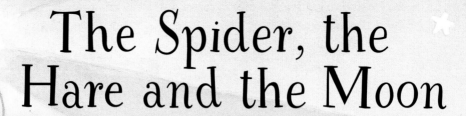

The Spider, the Hare and the Moon

The moon felt very sad. She knew that people on Earth were afraid of the dark, and she wanted to let them know that it was nothing to be scared of. She had no way of speaking to them herself, so she called on her friend the spider.

"Please take a message to everyone on Earth," she said to him. "Tell them that the world will always be in darkness at night, but there is no need to be afraid. I will be here to light their way."

The spider started to climb down the moonbeams to get back down to Earth. On the way, he bumped into the hare.

"Where are you going?" the hare asked.

"The moon has asked me to give an important message to all the people on Earth," the spider explained.

"Oh, you're so slow, it will take you much too long to get there," the hare said. "Let me take the message. I'm much faster than you. I'm sure if the moon said it was important she would want the people to hear it as quickly as possible. Tell me what the message is and I will give it to everyone on Earth."

"Well, I suppose the moon would want the people to hear her message as quickly as possible," the spider agreed. "Tell them the moon said that the world will always be in darkness …"

"Right," said the hare. "Tell the people on Earth that the world will always be in darkness."

And before the spider could finish, the hare had bounded off.

"Wait, wait," the spider shouted after him. "I haven't finished." But the hare had already disappeared.

The spider decided to go back and tell the moon what had happened. Otherwise she would wonder why the people on Earth were still scared.

Meanwhile, on Earth, the hare was busy telling all the people that the world would always be in darkness. And once he had delivered the message, he proudly went back to let the moon know what he had done.

Of course, the moon was furious with the hare – so furious in fact, that she sent him away and wouldn't speak to him ever again.

And the spider? The busy little spider is still trying to carry the moon's message to all the people on Earth as he spins his webs in the corners of our rooms.

Follow the Trail

Once upon a time there was a pair of tiger cub twins called Tia and Timus. They lived on the edge of the jungle with their mother. One day, Tia asked their mother if they could go down to the waterhole on their own.

"Yes," agreed Mother Tiger. "But don't stray from the path."

So Tia and Timus headed straight for the waterhole and played happily in the shallows. As they were splashing around, they heard something hissing in the undergrowth.

"Hey, it's a snake," cried Timus. "Let's go snake hunting."

"Yes," cried Tia, leaping out of the water. And, forgetting all about their mother's warning, the two tiger cubs went charging deep into the jungle. They raced on and on until they were quite out of breath.

"I don't think we'll ever find that snake, do you?" laughed Tia.

"No," agreed Timus. "And now I'm hungry and tired. Let's go home."

But when the tiger cubs looked around they discovered that they were quite lost.

"Oh, no," wailed Tia. "We'll never find the path again."

"We should have remembered Mummy's warning," cried Timus. The two cubs huddled together and trembled with fear.

They had heard all kinds of tales about the dangers that lurked in the jungle. Suddenly, Timus noticed something on the ground.

"Look," he cried. "We've left a trail of wet footprints. All we need to do is follow them and we'll find our way back to the waterhole."

"Then we'll be able to find the path leading home," added Tia.

So the two tiger cubs very carefully followed the footprint trail back to the waterhole. Then they followed the path all the way home. They didn't even stop when they heard something scratching around in a hollow tree trunk.

They were so pleased when they saw their mother that they bounced on her and gave her a big hug.

"Hey, what was that for?" asked Mother Tiger.

"Because we love you," said Tia.

"And you are so terribly wise," added Timus.

From then on, Tia and Timus always did exactly what their mother told them.

The Hare and the Tortoise

Once upon a time there was a hare who was always boasting about how fast he was.

One day, much to everyone's surprise, after Hare had been boasting even more than normal, Tortoise said, "Okay, Hare. I'll race you."

"Whaaaaat?" laughed Hare. "You've got to be joking." He laughed so much that he fell to his knees and thumped the floor with his fist.

"Tortoise, you're the slowest animal in the forest. I'll run circles around you!" he said.

There was a buzz of excitement in the forest the next morning.

"On your marks, get set… *go!*" cried the starting fox.

And Hare flew off at high speed, leaving a cloud of smoke where he had just stood. The tortoise trudged behind much, much, much more slowly.

Hare decided to take a quick look behind to see where the slow tortoise was. When he saw that Tortoise was far, far away, he decided to stop for breakfast. He feasted on some juicy carrots. Then he lay on his back, fiddled with his ears and yawned.

"This is just too easy," he said. "I think I'll have forty winks and catch up with him later." Soon he was fast asleep.

Tortoise plodded on and on. He got to where Hare was lying, fast asleep, and plodded past. He plodded on and on. Hare slept, on and on.

Suddenly Hare awoke with a jolt. He could just see Tortoise in the distance, plodding slowly and carefully towards the finish line.

"Nooooooo!" cried Hare. He leapt to his feet and charged towards the finish as fast as he could. But he was too late. Tortoise was over the line before him. Hare had been beaten.

After that, whenever anyone heard Hare boasting about his speed they reminded him about the day Tortoise beat him.

"Slow and steady won the race," they would say, laughing.

And all Hare could do was smile because, after all, they were quite right.